Teach me
TO PLEASE

Nera Stone

&

Nikki Black

Teach me to please @ 2023 Nera Stone & Nikki Black

Contents

A Note For The Readers

This novel is a work of fiction and contains

content intended for a mature audience only. Due to explicit language, foul language, graphic depictions of sex, and other triggers it may not be suitable for all readers.

-Thank you, Nera Stone & Nikki Black.

Authors Note

If you know us in person, this book will 100% make you think differently of me, so this is your only warning to turn back.

Content Warnings

Incest
Dual play
Face fucking
Rough sex
Cnc
Voyeurism
Bdsm/ sex clubs
Basically really dark and kinky so please beware

Chapter One

Rory

I can do this. I just need to take a deep breath and go in. I've been standing in this parking lot listening to the waves of the ocean crash for like ten minutes trying to work up the courage to enter the club but I don't know if I can. Especially because of the reason I'm here.

One month Prior

I glance over as I head up the driveway and realize my uncle must have stopped by. His gray Mercedes parked next to my dads informing me they're both here. As I enter the house, I make sure to take off my shoes and drop my bag down so that I can quickly go upstairs and begin writing the paper that is due tomorrow. However, as I turn to go to my father's

behind the cracked door. The sounds of groans and whimpers making me still. Just as I'm about to walk away I hear the sound of my dads voice. My body moving on it's own to peek inside while he speaks.

"Be a good girl darling, open that slutty little mouth for me so you can take us both. That's what you want to be for us isn't it? Our Good girl."

A whimper of a yes comes from some girl as she opens her mouth to take my dads cock. My eyes focus on his back as I move closer to look. All I can see is a girl on all fours between him and my uncle.

The uncle who is slamming into this unknown girl his chest on display and hands gripping her ass as he slams into her. I can't see much due to the position they're in but fuck. What I do know is this is wrong. I shouldn't be standing here watching this. And I definitely should be sliding my hand down and into my pants. But it's like I'm in a trance watching them both take this girl together. They're words dirty as they talk to her. Slipping my fingers under the band of my panties I let my fingers glide between my wet folds moving them in a slow circle against my clit as I watch them ravage her. God this is so wrong being this wet watching my dad and uncle fuck some girl but what's worse it just how bad I want to be her. They way they own her. Using her to please them. I want that, I want them to use me how they're using her. God what the fuck is wrong with me. Moving my fingers faster I slowly start to build up to an orgasm. My breathing becoming even with them as I wait to fall apart when they do. The girl comes with a scream as they let eachother know they're close. My fingers sliding down and pumping into my entrance ready to fall off the deep end with them. Just as they fall apart with a groan I move my free hand up to bite down on it as I fall apart. My eyes slowly opening as I ride it out on my hand. Only when they fully open they land back on my uncle. The uncle who seems to be staring straight at me, grin on his lips as I yank my hand from my pants. Before I even have time to think I'm darting down the stairs grabbing my bag and heading straight out the door. Shoes long forgotten I quickly search for my keys to escape. I don't even attempt to look back as I get into the car and drive off. I'm mortified that he caught me. I'm even more mortified that I enjoy the whole thing."

It's been exactly one month since I was caught and they haven't said a single thing to me. I'm not even sure Marcus told my dad. But one thing I do know is I need to watch again. As wrong as all of this is, it's like a craving. The need to just watch them one last time. Better yet feel it for myself. I know the second option won't happen but I at least need the first. So here I am Club Submerge, the local BDSM club down here in Crest Cove. The one marked down on my dad's calendar that I may or may not have snooped in. I guess uncle Marcus and him come here once a month to relieve some stress. Share a girl do what they do and then do it again the next month. I honestly tried my best to talk myself out of coming. But it's like this unscratched itch that I can't get rid of. I need to see it just one last time and then I'll never come back again. Try to get over this weird infatuation I now have developed.

Making my way through the entrance I slip on my mask aka part of the dress code and move over to the check in area. I applied for a membership the minute I saw his calendar. Did the background check and everything. I just wasn't sure if I was going to use it. Oh who am I kidding of course I was going to use it. I just had to work up the courage. Now I'm here checking in and now moving my way into the main club. I don't even know where they would be honestly. But the more into the club the person showing me around takes me the less confident I'm feeling. Maybe I should just turn around and leave. Try another time or better yet forget the whole thing. Before I have the chance to back out though it's like my eyes have a mind of their own just as they land on them. My body automatically drawn to their presence as they lead some girl into a room. Breaking me from my thoughts, the person guiding me around speaks.

"They're going into a viewing room if you want to watch. It's open to all."

Viewing room. I wonder if it's private or if they can see me if I watch. Like the person with me can read my thoughts, they speak again.

"They can't see you, only you can see them. It's totally up to you. I can show you some other popular spots as well if you'd like."

Shaking my head I speak up after what feels like forever.

"I'd like to watch them honestly if that's okay. Dip my toe in before I fall into the deep end if you know what I mean."

Nodding their head I watch as they walk away before I move towards the room they were talking about. Reading the door before I enter. To my left the activity room to my right the viewing area. Pushing open the right door I make my way in noticing that the room is luckily empty. Releasing the breath I didn't know I was holding I start to look around. My gaze landing on a giant window showing me into what seems to be a kind of bedroom only as I look inside I only see my uncle and some girl. My father nowhere in sight. Weird I could have swore I saw them all go in together. Maybe he's going to join them in a few.

Letting myself relax a little I watch as my Uncle avoids kissing the woman with him, his movements quick as he picks her up and throws her into the bed. She lets out a giggle before he's moving. His hand coming out to position her on all fours in an instant. My breath caught in my throat at the sight. He's naked. I know she is as well, but I'm not even paying any mind to her as I watch him move behind her. It feels like he knows I'm here. His eyes locking with mine as he slides his length into her. The sight familiar, reminding me of what I once watched before. The only difference being my dad isn't in there. Watching Uncle Marcus grip her hips he starts to slowly move his thrusts short as he fucks her.

Just before I can enjoy it too much a body is behind me. One hand on my throat before another comes to cover my mouth before I can scream or even put up a fight. A familiar voice whispers into my ear.

"Relax sweetheart it's just daddy. You think we wouldn't know you were here. That my brother wouldn't tell me what you saw. At first I was a little shocked that daddy's little girl stayed and watched us fuck our last little toy. But then I realized over the month watching you squirm under mine and Marcus's gaze what a perfect little doll you'd be for us. The way we could teach you how to please us the way we can please you. Yes this might be wrong morally but Honestly I could give a fuck less about that. Especially since we know once we have you there will be no one else. Now when I move my hand are you going to be a good girl and stay quiet."

Nodding my head against his hand I wait as he slowly removes both his hand from my throat and his other from my mouth. Both hands instantly moving to spin me to face him.

"Such a good girl. Now come with daddy and let's go join Uncle Marcus."

I don't even hesitate as I move with him. My body moving on its own like I'm a moth to a flame. Only this one I'm sure will burn me up. But I'm not sure I care.

Ganon-

I watch as my little girl follows me like a good little obedient thing. Her body hesitant as she moves but eager as well. She wants this as much as Marcus and I do. I honestly thought it would take more convincing. That I'd move my hand and maybe she'd yell. But they way her eyes glazed over. Her body instantly reacting to mine. She wants us just as bad and we plan to give her just what she needs. Leading her into the room I make sure to turn on the privacy switch letting everyone know there's no longer anything to watch as we make our way in. Moving her body in front of mine I make sure that both of us are fully inside the room before I'm shutting the door behind us. Her breathing grows uneven as she watches my brother, fuck some girl on the bed before us.

Automatically as we enter his eyes are on us, a smile pulling on his lips as he continues to thrust into the sub before him. Only his focus and attention isn't on her but on his sweet little niece instead. We thought this would be an easy way to break the ice. Let her have a show while I touch that sweet little pussy. Show her just what she's about to get herself into. What she'll never get to walk away from. Because once she's with us, that's it. She's ours for the taking.

Moving my body closer to hers, I bring my chest to her back. Watching her in the mirror on the other side as she lightly closes her eyes at the feeling. Moving one of my hands to her hips, I move the other up to wrap around her throat. Her eyes instantly shoot open. As I silently order her to watch. I want her to see what she's not only doing to my brother but also me. Grinding my hard cock into her ass, she starts to squirm at the site before her. Such an innocent little thing. I can't wait to break her. Make her only want and need us. Every pleasure given to her only by our touch or words. Ruin her for anyone ever again. Messed up to the point that all she'll ever want is us. Even if it's wrong in everyone else's eyes.

Marcus

Watching my little niece watch me fuck some sub has got to be one of the most erotic things ive ever experienced in my life. I honestly didn't think my dick could get any harder but it just goes to show she makes the impossible possible. Keeping my eyes locked on her I watch as my brother whispers something in her ear, her eyes locked on me the second he does. Her breathing growing shallower by the second. For a second I remember the Sub Im fucking who agreed to this all prior but honestly Its like she isnt even here, all I see is my little niece. All I feel is her. Well I wish it was her but I'll take her watching for now. Letting my eyes wander I follow the movement of my brother's hand as he slides it between her legs and right into her sweet little pussy. The wet sound of his fingers slowly pumping in and out of her driving me even crazier than I feel. His voice is low as he whispers to her, one hand gripping her jaw to watch as the other continues his pursuit to drive her to an orgasm. Wanting to get her there with me so we can fall over the edge together I go to speak up.

   "Such a sweet little sight watching my sweet little niece fall apart all over their daddy's fingers. Probably sucking him in like the good little girl you are. I bet you wish that was your daddy's fat cock in you don't you? That sweet little pussy swallowing him down while you beg to suck mine."

A loud moan falls from her lips, her body moving to ride his hand like she's chasing her climax.

Close.

She's so close and so am I.

Speaking up once again I wait for her to follow my command. Seeing how her body follows my orders.

"Come for us, Princess. Fuck your daddy's hand."
And just like the good little girl she is she falls apart
my climax washing over me seconds later as I watch
her fall apart while she rides my brothers fingers.
The sub beneath me coming with a scream
reminding me she's here. Pulling out of her she
waits for me to give her the okay to speak to me.
Nodding my head she thanks me for using her and
leaves us all alone.

Rory

Strong arms grip onto me harder not allowing me
to fall as I come down from my climax. That was
just, Wow. I must be in a daze because before I
realize the girl once in the room with us is gone and
I'm now in my dads arms. His lips coming down
onto my forehead before he pulls back to speak.

"I've got you baby. Rest. Uncle Marcus and I will take care of it all."

And they do. I know at some point we left the room. He spoke to the front desk person and got my things from the locker I put them in. Marcus taking my keys to drive my car home and my dad gently placing me in the car as we left. The last thing I remember is being lifted out, taken to my room, and tucked into bed. My lace mask slid off of me as they both kiss me goodnight, this time lightly on the lips.

Chapter Two

Rory

The morning sun filters through the curtains, casting a warm glow across the room. I groggily open my eyes, squinting against the bright light. The alarm clock on the bedside table goes off, signaling the start of a new day. I let out a sigh, my irritation mounting with each passing second as the thoughts from last night's events filter through my mind.

The sheets cling to me like a stubborn embrace, making my irritation grow even more. As I reluctantly swing my legs over the side of the bed, my feet meet the cool floor, a stark contrast to the warmth of the covers.

I rub my eyes, trying to shake off the remnants of dreams that cling to my consciousness. I slept like shit. Every time my eyes closed, Uncle Marcus and my dad filtered in, making me wish they never left me alone last night. The world seems out of focus, and my body protests with every movement. A glance at the clock tells me I'm running late for my morning class, which only fuels my annoyance.

The thought of facing them today looms over me like a storm cloud. With a grumble, I stumble towards the bathroom, my reflection in the mirror looking back at me with the same bleary-eyed distress. The shower, usually a sanctuary, offered little solace as the water's warmth failed to wash away my irritation.

Why did they leave last night? Why was I delivered to my bed after my dad finger fucked me at the club instead of him taking me to his room? At first, sleep came easy from the intense orgasm that my dad gave me, but it didn't last long until I was awake and couldn't find sleep again. I had half the mind to go find them and take what I wanted. What I still want. The thought that they might be rejecting me was too much. It made me nervous enough to stay in my bedroom, not even daring to step out the door until now.

Dressed in a hurry, I head downstairs with a heavy sigh. The aroma of freshly brewed coffee teases my senses, momentarily lifting my spirits. The kitchen, however, feels like an obstacle course. I fumble with the coffeemaker, cursing under my breath as I spill a few grounds in the process.

Finally, the rich, dark liquid began to fill the mug, and I stand there, waiting until I can finally leave. I feel like I'm suffocating with each second I'm here. Knowing any of them could walk through that door again at any time.

That's when a deep voice clears from behind me. My hands freeze and I can feel my heart begin to beat faster in my chest.

My goal was to escape unnoticed, but I guess that won't be happening. I square my shoulders with fake confidence and turn to face him.

My uncle Marcus leans against the door frame, his naked chest on display. I can't help but let my eyes wander down his body, a pair of gray sweatpants hanging low on his hips. The muscles bulge on his biceps as he crosses his arms, eyes roaming over me with hunger. When his eyes find mine, my thighs automatically press together. Marcus pushes off the door frame, stalking toward me as I take a step back. My ass hitting the counter behind me, halting me from moving away from him anymore.

"Rory," His deep voice hits my ears, causing my body to break out in goosebumps. That confidence I was faking once before is now long gone. I lower my eyes to the ground, suddenly feeling like a swarm of butterflies is starting a mosh pit in my stomach. Maybe last night was a bad idea. The need I have for him to put his hands on my body is the only thing I can think of. I know this is wrong, but I honestly can't help it.

Marcus grabs my face roughly, tipping my head back until our eyes clash. "What's got you so upset, Rory?" he asks, not releasing his tight grip on my face. He steps closer until his chest hits mine, leaving no room between us. A small thrill runs up my spine from his breath on my skin, but I can't get any words out before he starts speaking again.

"Is our little girl upset because she didn't get thoroughly fucked last night?" He chuckles and I grip the counter behind me until my knuckles turn white. He finally removes his grip from my face, his fingers moving toward the hem of my dress. "Was your dad's fingers not enough for our girl? I think you need to be filled with a big cock. Is that what you need, baby? Do you want your uncle to fuck that pretty little hole of yours?" Marcus's hungry gaze drops to my chest before his fingers ghost over my soaking wet center.

When his fingers make contact with my bare pussy, he hums his approval. "No panties, hmm?" My head shakes no on its own accord just as his fingers are gone. Like they were never there, just as my dad's tall frame steps through the kitchen door.

His eyes dart between his brother and me, a sinister smile on Marcus's face as he takes my coffee from the counter and takes a sip.

"Good morning," my dad's raspy morning voice hits my ears, and fuck if it doesn't send another wave of desire right through me. I can feel my juices dripping down my legs as I press them together once again.

Fuck, this is bad.

I give my dad a small smile. "Morning." I step over to where Marcus is leaning against the kitchen island and snatch my coffee out of his hand, bringing it up to my lips, moaning around the cup. Two sets of eyes swing my way and I take that as my cue to try to escape, but before I get the chance to, a strong set of arms wrap around my waist from behind, stopping me in my tracks. My body being spun around to face my dad once again. Marcus's mouth level with my ear as he speaks up from behind me.

"Not so fast, baby. Don't start something you didn't plan on finishing." My dad's heated gaze bores into mine and I can't help the whimper that slips past my lips when Marcus presses his hard length into my ass, showing me just how hard he is for me.

"Didn't we teach you better growing up? You should never start things you don't plan on finishing, Rory." My dad steps closer to me until I'm sandwiched between two strong men. Two hard cocks grinding into me from both sides. My hands come up to grip my dad's arms as my legs begin to shake from the neediness growing inside of me.

"Do we need to teach you how to finish a task?" his eyes leave mine only to look behind me at Marcus. I roll my eyes because not only am I seconds away from begging for them but what the hell do they mean by finish a task? They started something last night and left me wanting and needy all night long. "You think I need a lesson? What about you two? You fingered me only to leave me wanting more. All for you to not give me what I really want. So screw you both. I'm not the one who needs reminders on how to finish a task."

I instantly regret the words as soon as they left my mouth. My dad picks me up, throws me over his shoulder, and stalks out of the kitchen and right to the living room. My ass hits the soft cushion as I glare at my dad. Only for him to sit down next to me. He grips my waist and throws me on top of his lap.

Marcus kneels down where my face is pressed against the cushion and moves my fallen hair behind my ear. "So beautiful," he whispers before standing to his full height and sitting on the chair across from us.

I feel my dress being shoved up before a strong hand hits my bare ass causing me to scream out, my body squirming from the pain. I feel my dad's hard cock dig into my stomach.

The smacks to my ass don't stop as my screams get louder, tears stream down my face. "I want you to count for me, baby. We will do five more then I'll stop." My dad tells me as he runs his finger along the opening of my pussy and I moan. Another smack hits my ass and I cry harder. "I said count, Rory." my eyes land on Marcus and I sob into the cushion, desperate for someone to please me in any way.

"Please, Daddy," my voice is muffled as he smacks me again. "I said fucking count, Rory." My ass is so sore that I know I'll have bruises there tomorrow. And I can't wait to see. The thought of him marking me makes me feel feral.

"One," I give in and count.

"Two," *Smack*.

"Three," *Smack*.

"Four," *Smack*.

"Five,"

I've never been this wet in my entire life. My dad massages my ass until the pain eases away to just a light sting. Long fingers grip my thighs before spreading them until my glistening pussy is on display for him.

I reach up, wiping the tears from my eyes, and then look back at Marcus. His cock is in his hand as he strokes it. His hungry eyes never leave the spot where my Dad's fingers disappear inside of me.

My back arches on its own and my moans grow louder. I'm already close to coming but before I can, he pulls his hand away and I groan in protest.

"Daddy, Please. I need to come," I beg, but he doesn't grant my wish. "You're such a good girl, baby. There is one thing I need you to do before you can come," My dad helps me off his lap before pulling me with him across the room to where Marcus is still seated.

"Get on your knees, baby." Dad's hand pushes on my shoulder until my knees hit the carpeted floor and I can hear ringing in my ears. I can hear their words but I can't make out what they are saying as my nerves grow from what's going to happen.

"Rory," My uncle's warm palm on my cheek breaks me from my thoughts, my eyes meeting his now concerned ones. "We don't have to do this if it's not what you want, baby." his thumb brushes over my cheek and I lean into it, loving the way he cares if this is something I want.

"I want this. More than anything," I tell him truthfully. My dad kneels behind me, running a hand down the back of my hair, letting me know he's here with me.

"Good, now put your wet mouth on my cock, Rory. I need to feel how good you'll suck me down." my uncle says as his hand strokes his cock. I lean forward, taking his length into my mouth, swirling my tongue around the head of his cock. Marcus hisses through his teeth, his hand coming to guide me. "Fuck, baby." I begin to bob my head until the tip of his dick hits the back of my throat and I gag.

It doesn't take him long until he's taking over the small amount of control he handed over to me. His thrusts speed up and become more brutal. I can feel his length in my throat as my face hits his pubic area. His hips leave the couch to gain better access as the tears keep falling down my face and I can't breathe. "Fuck, you're taking me too well, baby. Does it turn you on that your Uncle is fucking your face, baby?"

Fingers find my clit and begin to move in slow measured circles and I could cry from that feeling alone.

Marcus leans forward and pinches my nose closed until stars dance in my vision, only then does he release my nose and pull his cock out of my mouth just as my dad sends me over the edge. I scream and collapse on Marcus's lap.

Panting and shaking.

My eyes close on their own accord just as a set of hands finds its way under my body. Gently lifting me from my place on Marcus's lap. "I love you, baby girl." my dad whispers into my ear as he takes us up stairs, straight into his room.

"Let's get you cleaned up," he says, Marcus following closely behind. "Okay," I mumble into his chest, not wanting to leave his arms. Marcus starts the shower as my dad places me on my feet. I sway from the lightheadedness that came with the intensity of what happened downstairs, but my dad is there to help steady me before my dress is being lifted from my body. My bra comes off next before Marcus takes my hand and leads us both into the shower. My dad tells us he will be waiting for us in the room with clean clothes.

"Let me wash you." His deep voice soothes me. Grabbing the body wash, he squeezes a decent amount in his hand before bringing it to my body. I can't help but lean back into his chest as his hands run over my pebbled nipples.

Once he finishes washing me, he fingers me until I cum, the water cold by the time we're done.

He turns off the water and steps out, holding a white fluffy towel in his hands for me. I step into it, enjoying the warmth it brings.

Marcus dries me off then hangs the towel on the hook. "Let's go get you in bed, Baby."

And with that, we exit the room, finding my dad seated on the end of the bed, one of his t-shirts in hand. Once he sees us emerge from the bathroom, he stands. Helping guide the shirt over my head, I let it fully slide on. Seeing it hangs down to mid-thigh, making me feel tiny in his giant shirt. A smile grows on my face at the thought.

Marcus is holding the blanket up for me to climb under before he leans down and presses his lips to mine. I can't help but try and deepen it but he doesn't let things get too far before he pulls back and stands up. My dad doing the same thing next.

"Goodnight, baby. We will see you in the morning and we'll talk." They both go to leave, but my voice comes out before I can even think of what to say.

"Don't go. Please stay with me," I basically beg, sitting up in the bed. They share a look with one another. Dad shrugs before grabbing the hem of his shirt and pulling it over his head. My mouth waters at the sight.

Marcus follows right behind him. After they both strip from their clothes, they climb into bed with me. One on each side.

I've never felt more safe than I do right now.

"Goodnight, Baby." is the last thing I hear before sleep takes me.

Chapter Three

Rory

Stirring I slowly start to wake to the sensation of fingers caressing my hair. My eyes fluttering open to find my Uncle Marcus's eyes on me. A small smile on his lips as he speaks. "Good morning Baby.

Sleep well? Ready to get that conversation done with?"

Letting a smile pull on my lips, I nod my head answering both questions he asked at once, as I let him help me up and off the bed. His fingers intertwine with mine as he leads me out of the room and into my dad's office. The man in question sitting behind the desk, glasses framing his face as he does some paperwork. The minute he sees us enter, he slowly slides them from his face as he speaks.

"Good Morning sleepy head. Ready to have our chat?"

Wanting to get this show on the road I release my hand from Marcus's as I make my way over to one of the chairs in front of his desk. Taking a seat with a deep sigh as I reply.

"Yes, sir."

My words make a mischievous smile spread on his handsome face, but before I can bask in it for too long. I hear the sound of my Uncle Marcus coming up behind my chair. My body instantly on alert around the pair of them. My dad uses that opportunity to draw my attention back to him as he clears his throat, his words serious as he speaks.

"Before we get to any sort of play I think it's important we have this discussion. Get everything out in the open. I'm going to tell you Rory what we want from you everything the two of us have discussed. And then you'll have the opportunity to say everything you want to, got it?"

Nodding my head, a look crosses his face as he corrects me.

"Words, baby."

The butterflies are back, my stomach a mess anytime the two of them call me that. I mean they always have but it's different now.

"Yes, sir. I understand."

That smile once before reappears making my stomach grow even wilder as we begin.

"Good girl."

Uncle Marcus's hands move to the back of my chair, the noise of him gripping it making me even more nervous as my dad speaks.

"We want you, baby. Not only as our little fuck toy but ours to keep. Like a relationship but the two of us with you. We'd be loyal to you as we'd expect you to be loyal to us. All the basic things in a relationship we'd do. This would be a forever kind of thing. Yes this is morally wrong to everyone around us. But No we don't care. We'd shield that all from you. Never let any of that get even close enough to touch you. But we must also warn you that if you say yes, that's it. You're ours for life so you must know we are a possessive and obsessive pair. Bad on our own, but even worse together. So think about this, everything I've just said. And then when you're ready, you can give us your answer."

Holy shit.

That was a lot. The only decision I am struggling to make right now is nothing to do with what he said but if I should tell them I want this. I don't want them to think that I'm desperate, that i've been thinking about this since the day I saw them fucking some girl in my dad's room. But fuck it. I want them and if telling them my answer right now gets them to fuck me I'm going to do it.

"I want this. I've already thought if you guys asked me what I would say. I want to be yours. A forever kind of thing."

A squeal leaves my lips as I'm being lifted from my chair. Uncle Marcus's hands under my arms lifting me. Pulling me back he presses his chest to my back as my dad gets up. His strides quick as he stops in front of me. Pressing his chest to mine so they have me sandwiched between them again.

 "How wet do you think our girl is Ganon?" Marcus says his husky words caressing my ear as he asks my dad.

Our Girl.

I'm theirs.

"I bet she's soaking. Aren't you, baby?"

 Not even giving me the chance to answer him, his body is sliding down in front of mine. His hands sliding under the hem of his shirt and lightly lifting it off of me. Leaving me naked in front of the pair of them.

 Continuing his pursuit down me I watch as he gets on his knees. His face becoming level with my pussy. Feeling myself grow wetter by the second, I'm honestly worried it's dripping down my legs at the sight. Feeling Marcus behind me take a step back I feel as his hands move down wrapping around my legs to lift me up. Spreading me wide open for my dad. He wastes no time as he's on me in an instant. His mouth is hot on my pussy as he starts to devour me. Slowly sucking my clit before he's moving down to dip his tongue into my entrance. Throwing my head back with a moan I let it rest on Marcus's shoulder as my dad brings me closer and closer to my orgasm. My words coming out way more needier than I intended.

"Please daddy. Please, please, please I need to come."

Pulling away his face is covered in my juices as a smirk spreads on his lips. His words full of heat and hunger as he speaks.

"Good girls deserve a reward and since you asked so nicely come for us, baby. Soak daddy's face."

And with that I come with a scream. My orgasm wracking my body as I shake in my Uncle's arms.

I don't even have time to really come down from it before my dads getting undressed, his naked body making my mouth water at the sight. For someone his age he really is in shape. And holy shit his cock is huge that's not going to fit inside of me. Still mid air my uncle lowers my feet to the floor, hands still on me as he makes sure I can stand before he's taking a step back. My body instantly missing the feeling of his just as I hear the sound of him getting naked behind me. It's like time moves at super speed as they're both naked, their hands instantly back on me. My body once again pressed between the both of them.

"You ready for us baby? Ready for Uncle Marcus and daddy to slide their cocks into your pretty little holes. Use you the way we want, teach you how to please us?"

The need building in me at my dads words is driving me insane. I want them to use me any way they want. Teach me to please. Anything to be their good girl.

"Yes please, daddy. Use me."

That's all they need as I'm being lifted once again. Only this time they're bringing me over to his couch, my body placed and bent over the edge giving my dad and Marcus the perfect setup for one to take me from behind the other my mouth. Just how they used the girl when I caught them. For some fucked up reason that makes me even needier. Knowing they're going to use me how I first saw them. Just how this all started.

Marcus moves behind me in an instant, my dad coming to my front so his cock is level with my mouth.

They waste no time as they both line up with each entrance. My Uncle's words driving me crazy as they both slide into me.

"Such an obedient little fuck toy she is. Isn't she Ganon?"

He answers him as his hands slide into my hair. Using my face to please him how he wants.

"Such a good fuck toy. Our sweet little girl, so eager to please. And fuck you were right her mouth is heaven on earth."

Picking up the pace my Uncle's hands grip my hips hard as he starts to thrust into me harder. My dad giving me no room as he brutally fucks my throat. They do exactly what they promised before using me just how they want. And god it has me on the edge so close to exploding it's insane. I've never come from penetration but with them, I'm just about to.

Feeling Marcus start to grow ridged, my dad breathing growing shallower I know they're there with me. All of us ready to fall apart.

And like they know I am as well, my dad speaks his words husky as they come out.

"I'm close and I know you both are as well. Come for us baby fall apart all over your uncle's cock. Drink me down like the good little come guzzler you are."

And we do. I'm the first to come with a scream around my dads cock as Ganon is next, his cock filling my just as my dads does. Hot spurts of cum shooting all down my throat. And just like the good girl I promised to be, I swallow every little drop like he told me to. Both of them slowly start to pull themselves free.

My body about to hit the couch before my uncle's hands catch me. Honestly, the rest is all a blur as my body is being lifted and taken back into my dad's room. My mind empty and body content as they both once again get into bed with me. I wasn't even up that long before they fuck me back to sleep.

Chapter Four

Ganon

Rory is asleep when the sound of the front door is being opened. Making my way out of the room and down the stairs I watch as my ex wife Clara lets herself in as if she still lives here. Which she's about to find out she can't just do anymore. This is it.

She's not going to hurt Rory anymore with her disappearance act. Showing up when her last relationship doesn't work out to try to temporarily get back with me. Not gonna happen. I meant what I said when I told Rory that Marcus and I want this forever. Wrong as it is, she's ours and she's stuck with us. Not that she's mad about that anyways. Hearing steps behind me I know that Marcus has joined me as we get ready to confront Clara.

Hitting the bottom of the steps her eyes shoot to us as a smile takes over her face. Her annoying ass voice reaching my ears as she speaks.

"Hello handsome. I sure as hell missed that good looking face of yours. Where's my things that were down here?"

What's the most aggravating in the situation is that she still thinks that I'm just gonna keep her things around. That she can come as she pleases, and I will always just be there to take her back. She's not going to like what I have to tell her today. Definitely gonna ruin her mood. Oh well not my problem.

 "Clara. Your things are all boxed in the garage you can grab them now but seeing how much shit you have I think it would be best to get movers to move them. I am more than happy and willing to arrange and pay for that. Just let me know when you want to get them and to where you want them delivered." It's actually funny/comical at how wide her mouth is hanging open. Like she didn't expect me to kick her out. My ex wife. The woman who cheated on me and I divorced.

 Seeing that she's not gonna say anything I go to move around her. Only as I stepped to the side, her hand reaches out to grab the top of my arm. Marcus ready to step in and intervene only I waive him off. Not wanting this to become bigger than it needs to be.

"What did I do baby. I know that we've had our ups and downs, but kicking me out really. We're good together. Hell I'll even let Marcus join."
That definitely ticked him off As I hear him mudder under his breath.

"Like I ever wanted her whore ass. Be forreal."
She sends him a glare over her shoulder as she continues trying to Convince me to let her stay.

"You know you still love me baby. So what is it? Is there another whore? Are you sleeping with somebody else? Even worse, are you doing it with Marcus?"
I wonder if she understands how stupid she sounds when she talks. She basically just insinuated that she was a whore. Which she also seconds prior tried to get with both Marcus and I and now she's making it sound like it's a disgusting thing.

Before this can go any further, The sound of footsteps pull all of our attention to the stairs. A sleepy, looking Rory making her way down in nothing but my shirt Probably coming to find out what the commotion is. Marcus tries to head up the stairs, a little bit stopping Rory in her tracks. Telling her that she doesn't want to hear this. But that only makes her want to continue her pursuit as she tells him she deserves to hear what's going on. And as she hits the middle of the stairs Clara chooses that moment to speak up.

"So the whore Is my own daughter. Really Ganon. You and Marcus are both fucking sick." Before I can let her say, too much or anything that will hurt Rory's feelings. I cut her off. Keeping to My promise to Rory that I'll never let this shit touch her.

"Don't start Because I'll let it all fall. Tell her who exactly you cheated on me with that caused us to divorce in the first place. Yours being even worse because it broke up a family."

The color drains from her face as she realizes that I'll drop the bomb. Tell everyone in this room who she cheated on me with, something that she doesn't want to touch The light of day. Scowl on her face she turns ready to stomp her way out the door before she speaks up one last time.

"I'll Let you know when I plan to get my shit picked up. I'll keep my mouth shut if you keep yours. Have fun fucking our daughter."

And with that, she slams the door. The sound of Rory's footsteps, running up the stairs, making me curse under my breath. She just had to do that shit today. Right when we got our girl to be ours. Marcus speaks up as he starts to make his way up the stairs.

"I got this. You make sure that wench is gone. I'll take care of our girl. Join us when you're done."

Nodding my head, he makes his way up the rest of the stairs as I turn to lock the door to make sure that she's completely gone.

Marcus

Following Rory up the steps it breaks my heart as I hear the little sniffles coming from our girl. Anger taking over me that Clara had the audacity to come in here and stir shit it up In the first place. She doesn't think anybody knows but my brother, but he told me when they got divorced, who she cheated on him with. And the only reason why she won't say anything about us seeing she's in the same boat. The first man that she got with being her brother before she moved onto scamming men to pay for her lifestyle. And like every time before this one she shows up when it doesn't work out, trying to get Ganon back, not that he would take her back anyways, but she sure tries. The minute he doesn't fall for her shit she then moves onto the next guy. What pisses the two of us off is that the one person she's hurting the most throughout all of this is Rory. When she left she hurt her the most and when she comes back and tries to play family for a small amount of time she doesn't realize she hurts her the most, or if she does she just doesn't care.

Last visit Rory finally decided to end whatever relationship they had and her mom proved it a good choice by just agreeing and telling her it's her choice. But that's the past problems, right now I'm worried that she listened to her moms words or worse thinks that Ganon is going to give her a shot. He would never but I need to make sure she knows that. I need to know where her head is at.

Rory

I hate this. I hate her. I can hear the footsteps of what I'm assuming is Marcus following me in my attempt to escape to my dads room. Only just as I enter his hand is on my arm spinning me to face him. My eyes glassy as I try to keep my tears in.

"Oh baby. Please don't listen to a word she said. If you think your dad is going to choose her, know that she was and never will be a choice he'll make. You're all he sees. Fuck your all that we see. Our girl. Tell me what's wrong baby. Let me in."
The tears I was once holding in or at least trying to are now pouring down my face. His words warming as I spill it all. Tell him every little thing hoping he'll be there to hold me together as I break.

"I hate her. I hate that she thinks she can walk in and out of our life's like we mean nothing. Just a spot for her to rest her bags before she's off again. I just wish she'd never come back, never contact us and just disappear from our life's all together." Using his thumb to wipe away my tears. I let myself melt into his touch, my face pushing into his chest as he places a kiss on top of my head. His words warm and loving as he consoles me.

"I'm so sorry she is who she is baby. But your dad and I made a promise to keep the bad away from you and obviously we're doing a shitty start but from this day forward you will never have to deal with her or any other problem like that again. You're ours to keep, our to protect. And we will make sure she won't ever get to hurt you again." Snuggling further into him I let his words crush everything she's ever said and done to me. The feeling of his arms around me reminding me that I

have and will always have them. I will always be
their girl.

Ganon

Walking into the room and hearing my little girl
sniffle because of something her mother did or said
is breaking my heart. The thought that I let that
bitch even close enough to breathe the same air as
her is something I'll always have to live with. It will
never happen again. She is gone and this time it's
for good. She knows the consequences if she isn't.

Walking closer my brother looks up, his eyes
locking with mine as he holds our girl. Letting me
know that he handled it but I still need her to know
that it won't happen again. That she won't ever cry
over her again.

"Baby."

I wait for her to look up, her head leaving Marcus's chest as she turns to look at me, tears still in her eyes.

"Come here."

It takes her less than two seconds to come running into my arms. Her cry's coming out a little harder as I whisper reassuring words to her. My lips finding the top of her head as I speak again. Her cries quieting as I start to talk.

"I'm so sorry baby. I should have better protected you and kept her away from you but it won't happen again. She'll never have the chance to breathe the same air as you again. Daddy and Uncle Marcus will never let anything close to hurting you ever again."

Cutting me off she puts her hand over my mouth stopping the rest of my speech. My eyebrow raising in question at her boldness.

"Shhh it's not your fault. Either of yours. It's just seeing her brings up all the hurt she brings and starting today I'm not going to let her hurt me anymore. Not when I have you guys. Forever." Kissing the inside of her hand Marcus chooses that moment to talk.

"Forever baby."

My words next as she moves her hand from my mouth.

"Forever Princess. You have us forever."

Gifting me with a sweet little smile I grow hard at the sight. I like her like this, a smile finding her lips, lust filling her eyes. She must just notice our half nakedness because her eyes roam the two of us as she backs up. Taking in Marcus and I's bare chested states her breathing growing shallower. I think it's definitely time to get our girls mind off of everything.

Chapter Five

Rory

I don't even get a chance to take anything in before his lips are on mine. My dad consuming me with his kiss, while my Uncle comes up from behind to sandwich me in between them.

My dads breaking the kiss to lower his head whispering in my ear as my Uncle's hands continue to roam my body.

"Now it's time to be a good girl for daddy and Uncle Marcus. Time to do what we've been teaching you. Go ahead make Uncle Marcus feel good and then we can have some daddy daughter time. Okay baby?"

Nodding my head slowly I watch as he pulls back my Uncle spinning me to now face him. His lips replacing my fathers from moments prior in an all consuming kiss.

His grip on me is harsh as he moves us over to the bed. Both of us naked in seconds as he removes his sweats, my dads shirt once covering my body lifted over my head as he takes a step back to get a better view.

"Fuck, baby if I wasnt hard before this in itself would have me hard as a rock in seconds. Our little girl all grown up and all ours to do with as we please."

The whiny little noise that escapes my throat from his words sends a look of heat or hunger through his eyes. His body once again pressed to mine as he guides me to the edge of the bed. My eyes go to look for my dad only before I can. He's gripping my chin, Uncle Marcus's words firm as he demands my attention.

"Eyes on me baby. You'll have your fun with him later, right now it's just you and me, Understand?"

Nodding my head, his grip on my chin tightens.

"Words little girl."

My breath catches at his choice of words. How fucked up is it that I get wetter than I should when my dad and Uncle call me names like that? That being with them or having them look at me the way they do turns me on so much. Wrong or not, I love it.

Pulling myself from my thoughts I quickly speak up trying to not show just how much his words affect me. But I'm pretty sure he can see right through me as a smirk starts to pull on his face.

"Yes sir."

Laying a light kiss on my lips he doesn't release my chin as he pulls back a smirk still on his face.

"Good girl."

Before I even have time to react to his words again, he's moving away. Sitting on the bed he leans against the headboard. His hand extended out inviting me to sit in his lap. Taking it I let him move me how he wants. His hands positioning me to hover right on top of his cock. My body moving on its own as I slide down onto him.

"Fuck baby, your sweet little pussy is sucking me down so fucking good. I could bust just like this. Move for me, baby. Take what you want."

His breathy words heighten my arousal as I do exactly what he asked, taking what I want and riding him slowly. I love the groans and noises coming from him as I work him. The sound of his cock sliding into my wetness making me want to drag this out for as long as I possibly can. Only my mind is drawn to the other side of the room as I hear other groans. My dad sitting in the chair in the corner of the room. I know I'm supposed to be focused on Marcus but the sounds from the both of them are driving me insane. The thought that my dad is getting off to me riding his brother has me moving faster. My head falling back in a moan as my clit grinds against the base of my Uncle's cock. His hands now moving to grip my hips as he thrusts into me.

"Fuck baby I'm going to come and the sweet little pussy of yours is going to swallow every little drop. And like the good little girl you are, you're going to go over there and ride my brother and let him fill you up next aren't you baby?"

Picking up my pace I start to ride him faster as my words come out as a moan.

"Yes, please sir. Fill me up. I want to feel you both inside me."

And he does exactly that. His thrusts brutal before he's filling me up. His cock coating my womb as he continues to fuck me through his orgasm. My own washing over me and he comes down from his. Slowing my movements I let my eyes once again wander to my dad, his hand still working himself before he's speaking, up his words more of a command than an invitation.

"Come to daddy baby."

Snapping my attention back to my Uncle Marcus, his grip on me tightens as he helps me off of him. His smile telling me to do what my dad says. Making my way over I come to a stop between his legs, his hand once stroking himself moving to grip my hip just like my Uncle did.

"You're going to ride daddy just like you did so sweetly for Uncle Marcus. Then when daddy is going to come your sweet little pussy is going to take every little drop like the good little fuck toy it is. After that, we'll put our sweet little girl to bed. You got it, baby?"

Just as he gives me guidance on what he wants me to do, I can't help but let my words slip free. His tone leaving no room for argument.

"Yes, daddy."

Smile on his lips, he does the same thing his brother did as his hand comes out to guide me to get on top of him. His grip hard as me moves me just over the tip of his cock. Giving me all the power as I slide onto him.

"Fuck baby you feel so fucking good. Your cunt is gripping me so well. Definitely made just for the two of us."

Gripping him tighter I love the groan that escapes his lips as I go to start to move my hips. The only thing that's different is that he uses his grip on my hips to direct me instead of letting me move on my own. His hands working me in a way that pleases him. His breathing let me know he's close, I'm honestly surprised he lasted this long since he's been working himself since earlier. Waiting so he could come with me. And like I can read his mind or something, he speaks up, his movements growing rougher.

"I'm close baby. Come with me. Cum all over daddy's cock."

His words have some sort of magic in them because the minute he tells me what to do my body reacts. My orgasm washing over me like a tidal wave, my vision black as he basically makes me see stars. His own climax coming soon after, pumping me full of his cum. I must pass out at some point because the minute my body hits the bed both my dad and Marcus speak up. A blanket wrapped around me as they do.

"Goodnight baby. Sweet dreams. We love you."
My dad speaking next.

"Goodnight little girl. We love you and we're so happy you chose to be our girl."
My words coming out sleepy and they die off.

"I love you both too. Thank you for choosing me and teaching me to please. Goodnight."

THE END

Thank you Page

Thank you for giving these books a try and for being the dirty little readers you are. You all truly are the best.

Acknowledgement

To everyone who loves the dirty twisted taboo stories this is for you.

About the Authors

Social Media Platforms- @AuthorNerastone & @AuthorNikkiBlack
The Authors are a part of the book community and you may find further information about them on social media Platforms.

Next In The Series

Last book But maybe a new series to come.

Others In the series

Teach me to please
Teach us a lesson

Printed in Great Britain
by Amazon

43138636R10050